This book belongs to

_____

The Complete Adventures of Curious George

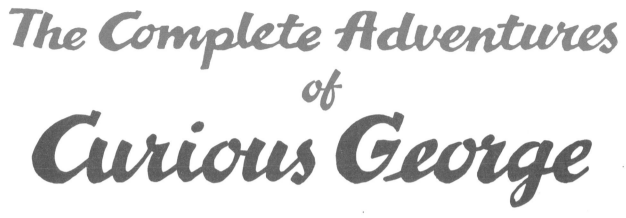

MARGRET & H. A. REY

Houghton Mifflin Company
Boston

Manufactured in the United States of America
DOW 10 9

Contents

An illustration from the original Curious George

Introduction

Curious George, quintessential childhood tale of monkeyshines and mischief, was the creation of wartime refugees who knew, better than George himself, what it meant to escape by the seat of one's pants. A self-taught artist, Hans Augusto Rey (1898–1977) and his Bauhaus-trained wife and collaborator, Margret (1906–1996), were German Jews who met and married in Brazil in 1935. After cofounding the first advertising agency in Rio de Janeiro, they returned to Europe in 1936, remaining in Paris until just hours before the German army entered the French capital on June 14, 1940. Then, fleeing by bicycle with their winter coats and several picture books strapped to the racks (including the watercolors and a draft of the as-yet-unpublished *Curious George*—then called *Fifi*), they crossed the French-Spanish border, caught a train bound for Lisbon, and then sailed to Brazil. Hans's Brazilian passport and Roosevelt's Good Neighbor Policy eased the couple's passage to the United States.

As a university student in Germany, Hans Rey had read philosophy and natural sciences and mastered several languages. It was largely by chance that this restless polymath, who also had a knack for drawing, embarked on a career in children's books. When an editor at the French house Gallimard admired his animal illustrations for a Paris newspaper, Rey, who was then in his thirties, responded by submitting the picture book later published in the United States as *Cecily G. and the 9 Monkeys* (Houghton Mifflin, 1942). The French *Cecily* marked not only Rey's debut in the field but also the first appearance of Curious George (who, under the name "Fifi," figures in the story as one of the nine). As more books for Gallimard followed, Rey also established a foothold in Britain, where Grace Hogarth, an American employed in London as Chatto & Windus's children's book editor, took an interest in his work. When wartime considerations prompted both Hogarth and the Reys to plan on resettling in the States, the editor secured from Hans the promise of a first look at whatever projects he might bring over with him.

Soon after the couple's arrival in New York, in October 1940, Hogarth, who had assumed the editorship of Houghton Mifflin's newly formed children's books department, came down from Boston to inspect the artist's wares. At canny Margret's insistence, Hogarth agreed to a then rare four-book contract. It was thus that in the fall of 1941 Houghton Mifflin published *Curious George* (the new title was the publisher's happy idea) as well as a novelty book called *How Do You Get There? Cecily G. and the 9 Monkeys* and a second lift-the-flap book, *Anybody at Home?,* followed a year later. (In 1942, Chatto & Windus issued the first British edition of *Curious George* under yet another title, *Zozo:* George was the reigning monarch's name, and in 1940s Britain, *curious* meant "gay.")

Margret, who was a famously tenacious negotiator, continued to mind the couple's business affairs while writing books of her own and contributing substantially to her husband's creative efforts as ad hoc art director and sometime coauthor. On occasion she even posed for drawings of George. In social situations, Hans typically made the gentler impression: when he roared like a lion, it was most often to make visiting children laugh. Nonetheless, Rey the artist was a steely perfectionist. In Paris, he had worked closely with the skilled artisans responsible for the printing of his books. To accommodate his wish to do so again, Hogarth chose a suitable New York printer, William Glaser, specialist in fine color work.

Rey may have assumed at first that his original watercolors were destined for reproduction by the same exacting—and costly—photolithographic process favored in Europe. Thrifty American publishers, however, reserved photolithography for picture books assured of a substantial sale, and Rey had arrived in the United States an unknown. Moreover, the manager of the trade department and Hogarth's superior, Lovell Thompson, had concluded that the watercolors for *Curious George* looked "as if the author still planned to point them up . . . and clean them up [in places]." Thompson ruled that a new set of "pre-separated" illustrations based on the watercolors should instead be prepared.

Whatever Rey's own first thoughts on the subject may have been, he quickly adapted to circumstance, as well as to the more graphic, less painterly aesthetic implicit in the method of reproduction made available to him. In preparing the separations for *Curious George,* Rey served a whirlwind apprenticeship, over the course of which he transformed a technique foreign to him into a uniquely expressive idiom for his art.

Curious George appeared to strong reviews on the same Houghton Mifflin list as Holling C. Holling's *Paddle-to-the-Sea* (which far outsold it up until the early 1950s) and in the same season as Robert McCloskey's *Make Way for Ducklings* (Viking), which won the year's Caldecott Medal. The attack on Pearl Harbor followed later that same fall, and with the United States' entry into World War II came paper rationing and other wartime restrictions that severely limited the potential sale of most children's books.

Curious George's fortunes rose with the birthrate during the postwar baby boom years. One of the book's first reviewers had predicted that small children would "wear the book out with affection." With time and the publication of six sequels, Rey's spry mischief-maker came to occupy a permanent place in our collective imagination, a near relation to Dr. Seuss's Cat in the Hat, Don Freeman's Corduroy, and Maurice Sendak's Max. Sixty years after he first endeared himself to the mild-mannered man with the yellow hat, George remains a bright standard-bearer for the universal curiosity of children: their large-as-life need to touch and tangle with the world and to learn by doing— even if to do so means occasionally landing in thickets of trouble.

Over the years, the Reys, who had no children of their own, remained unaffected by their steadily growing fame and fortune. They continued to work hard and live modestly, first in New York's Greenwich Village and later in Cambridge, Massachusetts, and to lend their support to causes in which they believed, such as the civil rights movement. From time to time, typically at intervals of five or so years, they returned to their favorite character to tell a new story about him.

More often than not, the Reys had something up their sleeve. *Curious George Gets a Medal* (1957), in which George goes for a ride in a rocket, was published, presciently, weeks before the Soviets' surprise launch of the *Sputnik II* satellite, which carried the first animal into space (a small dog named Laika). Hans Rey, long fascinated by the prospects for space travel, had wished to share his enthusiasm for rocketry with the young. Then, a year after Dr. Seuss's *Cat in the Hat* popularized the practice for storybooks, Margret Rey wrote *Curious George Flies a Kite* (1958) with a "controlled," or simplified, vocabulary aimed at helping children learn to read. *Curious George Goes to the Hospital* (1966) was conceived in part as an aid in preparing children for first-time hospital stays.

The Reys, however, took care not to allow their nobler intentions to overwhelm their beloved little monkey's blithely madcap appeal. From the first book to the last, George remains the most entertaining of characters—the ultimate innocent and incorrigible clown. For Hans and Margret Rey there was lesson enough for readers in the threadbare margin by which George survives his more spectacular pratfalls. Had not the couple learned a similar lesson, in a far darker key, themselves, cycling at the last possible moment through enemy lines in Occupied Europe toward an uncertain future nearly half a world away?

For Curious George's creators, to land on one's feet was always the first order of business: the rest was joy.

—Leonard S. Marcus

Curious George
A Publisher's Perspective

By any standard of publishing, the Houghton Mifflin children's list of 1941 was a very fine list indeed. About twenty books saw publication that year; six stayed in print for about two decades, three still remain. The list was the work of Grace Hogarth, one of England's great children's book editors, who had come to live in Boston during the war. She convinced the Houghton management that the house needed a children's book department, such as those that existed in many British and American firms. She started the department, trained Lee Kingman Natti to succeed her, and managed to publish some of America's classic authors and books before returning to England after the war.

On October 18, 1940, Grace wrote to H. A. Rey in New York, saying, "I am, as you know, keen on all your books." But in a later letter she acknowledged that she had never seen *Fifi,* the original French version of *Curious George.* By modern standards, Ms. Hogarth moved with lightning speed. On November 7, she informed the Reys that she would give them a contract for four titles, with an advance of $1,000—probably one of the most well spent $1,000 in all of publishing history. "Keen," Grace Hogarth may have been, but she protected Houghton's finances with an eagle eye. H. A. Rey accepted the $1,000, but noted that it was "considerably lower" than advances he had received in England and France. By November 13, both the print run of *Curious George* at 7,500 copies and the price of $2.00 or less had been established. A week later the publication date of August 1941 had been set. Perhaps with a small list and few staff members, such decisions came even more quickly than would be possible in our high-speed technological age. Grace Hogarth would have preferred to publish *Raffy* (*Cecily G. and the 9 Monkeys*) first, but, as she wrote, "It has occurred to us that by 1942 the Nazis may be out of Paris, in which case we might be able to buy sheets of *Raffy* from Gallimard [the French publisher]." And therefore, *Curious George* became the first Rey picture book offered in the United States.

But it is only by happy circumstance that we can celebrate the birthday of George at all. He might well never have come into being. He was, after all, smuggled out of Paris on a bicycle as his creators fled the Nazis in 1940. Although *Curious George* was published to strong sales, three other 1941 titles, Holling C. Holling's *Paddle-to-the-Sea*, Virginia Lee Burton's *Calico*, and Richard Hubler's *Lou Gehrig*, all outshone George in book sales for many years. Laudatory but unexceptional reviews greeted the book; *Horn Book* called the saga "a satisfying funny book," but gave more praise to other titles, which have long since vanished from the canon of children's books.

In 1945, in fact, *Curious George* had sold negative-six copies; bookstores returned more than they bought that year. Many books with this kind of selling record have been and are still being put out of print at such a moment in their history. But Houghton continued to support the Reys and George through six more titles. Grace Hogarth and her successors had taken a shine to the insouciant little monkey, as had children themselves. Eventually, early readers of George began to pass down the books to their own children. In 1958 *Curious George* managed to sell over 10,000 copies in a year for the first time. Today, close to 25 million copies of the Curious George titles are in print. Few children's books ever stay in print for a decade. At six decades, George's story remains more vital than most that will be brought into print this year.

As human beings, the Reys were as remarkable as the character they created. Hans was a genius with children. I once saw him entertain an auditorium with probably five hundred children brought in by school bus to Boston for the day. I could have heard a pin drop as he drew and talked, a man as modest and gentle as his character. Margret, a force to be reckoned with in the universe, had served as Hans's model for Curious George and was unfailingly direct and curious herself. She could make grown men weep, and could—and did—terrorize her publishers. I would pick up the phone to hear Margret's voice saying, "You always wear hats, Anita. Is there something wrong with your head?" And, of course, because she demanded an answer, I could only reply, "Nothing, Margret, that a hat can hide." When those who worked with her get together, we still tell Margret stories—she left a memory of her spirit and her courage with us all.

As Margret lay dying she called many of her friends and colleagues, in turn, to say goodbye. The last time I saw her, she was in her bed, too weak to talk much but still very present. She held my hand and sang in German. As I sat with her, I had a vision of Margret as a girl, speaking the language of her ancestors. She had always remained close to that child, as had Hans to the child within him. Now Hans, Margret, and their books belong to the ages. But their most enduring creation, Curious George, lives on—an ever-mischievous young monkey, beloved by children for sixty years.

—Anita Silvey
Westwood, Massachusetts

Curious George

This is George.
He lived in Africa.
He was a good little monkey
and always very curious.

One day George saw a man.
He had on a large yellow straw hat.
The man saw George too.
"What a nice little monkey," he thought.
"I would like to take him home with me."
He put his hat on the ground
and, of course, George was curious.
He came down from the tree
to look at the large yellow hat.

The hat had been on the man's head.
George thought it would be nice
to have it on his own head.
He picked it up and put it on.

9

The hat covered George's head.
He couldn't see.
The man picked him up quickly
and popped him into a bag.
George was caught.

The man with the big yellow hat
put George into a little boat,
and a sailor rowed them both
across the water to a big ship.
George was sad, but he was still
a little curious.

On the big ship, things began to happen.

The man took off the bag.

George sat on a little stool and the man said,

"George, I am going to take you to a big Zoo

in a big city. You will like it there.

Now run along and play,

but don't get into trouble."

George promised to be good.

But it is easy for little monkeys to forget.

On the deck he found some sea gulls.
He wondered how they could fly.
He was very curious.
Finally he HAD to try.
It looked easy. But—

oh, what happened!
First this—

and then this!

"WHERE IS GEORGE?"
The sailors looked and looked.
At last they saw him
struggling in the water,
and almost all tired out.

"Man overboard!" the sailors cried
as they threw him a lifebelt.
George caught it and held on.
At last he was safe on board.

After that George was more careful
to be a good monkey, until, at last,
the long trip was over.
George said good-bye to the kind sailors,
and he and the man with the yellow hat
walked off the ship on to the shore
and on into the city to the man's house.

After a good meal
and a good pipe
George felt very tired.

He crawled into bed
and fell asleep at once.

The next morning
the man telephoned the Zoo.
George watched him.
He was fascinated.
Then the man went away.

George was curious.
He wanted to telephone, too.
One, two, three, four, five, six, seven.
What fun!

DING-A-LING-A-LING!
GEORGE HAD TELEPHONED
THE FIRE STATION!
The firemen rushed to the telephone.
"Hello! Hello!" they said.
But there was no answer.
Then they looked for the signal
on the big map that showed
where the telephone call had come from.
They didn't know it was GEORGE.
They thought it was a real fire.

HURRY! HURRY! HURRY!
The firemen jumped on to the fire engines
and on to the hook-and-ladders.
Ding-dong-ding-dong.
Everyone out of the way!
Hurry! Hurry! Hurry!

The firemen rushed into the house.

They opened the door.

NO FIRE!

ONLY a naughty little monkey.

"Oh, catch him, catch him," they cried.

George tried to run away.

He almost did, but he got caught

in the telephone wire, and—

a thin fireman caught one arm
and a fat fireman caught the other.
"You fooled the fire department,"
they said. "We will have to shut you up
where you can't do any more harm."
They took him away
and shut him in a prison.

39

George wanted to get out.
He climbed up to the window
to try the bars.
Just then the watchman came in.
He got on the wooden bed to catch George.
But he was too big and heavy.
The bed tipped up,
the watchman fell over,
and, quick as lightning,
George ran out through the open door.

He hurried through the building
and out on to the roof. And then
he was lucky to be a monkey:
out he walked on to the telephone wires.
Quickly and quietly over the guard's head,
George walked away.
He was free!

Down in the street
outside the prison wall,
stood a balloon man.
A little girl bought a balloon
for her brother.
George watched.
He was curious again.
He felt he MUST have
a bright red balloon.
He reached over and
tried to help himself, but—

instead of one balloon,
the whole bunch broke loose.
In an instant
the wind whisked them all away
and, with them, went George,
holding tight with both hands.

47

Up, up he sailed, higher and higher.
The houses looked like toy houses
and the people like dolls.
George was frightened.
He held on very tight.

At first the wind blew in great gusts.
Then it quieted.
Finally it stopped blowing altogether.
George was very tired.
Down, down he went—bump,
on to the top of a traffic light.
Everyone was surprised.
The traffic got all mixed up.
George didn't know what to do,
and then he heard someone call,
"GEORGE!"
He looked down and saw his friend,
the man with the big yellow hat!

George was very happy.
The man was happy too.
George slid down the post
and the man with the big yellow hat
put him under his arm.
Then he paid the balloon man
for all the balloons.
And then George and the man
climbed into the car
and at last, away they went

to the ZOO!

What a nice place
for George to live!

Curious George takes a Job

This is George. He lived in the Zoo.

He was a good little monkey and always very curious.

He wanted to find out what was going on outside the Zoo.

One day, when the keeper was not paying attention,
George got hold of the key for the cage.

When the keeper discovered what had happened, it was too late — George was gone!

WHERE WAS GEORGE?
They looked for him everywhere.

But they could not find him.

George was hiding in the hay of his friend, the elephant.
Finally the keepers gave up looking for him.

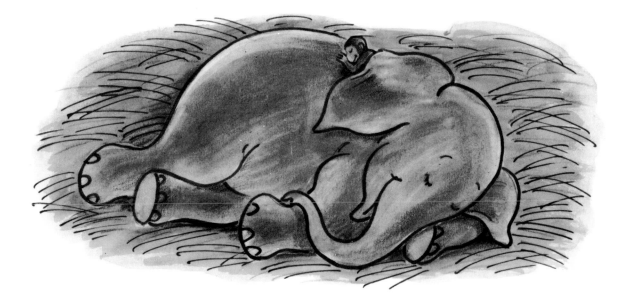

George found a nice cozy spot to sleep under the elephant's right ear, and the next morning, before the Zoo opened, he got away safely.

Once in the street George felt a little scared. What should he do in the big city? Maybe he could find his friend, the man with the yellow hat, who had brought him over from Africa a long time ago. Only George did not know where he lived.

There was a bus stopping at the corner. George had never ridden on one. Quickly he climbed a lamp post, jumped on top of the bus and off they went.

Now they were right
of the town. There was
that George did not know
If only he could go on riding

in the center
so much to see
where to look first.
like this forever!

But after a while George got tired and a little dizzy.

When the bus slowed down to turn into a side street, George jumped off.

There was a restaurant right in front of him. Mmmm — something smelled good! Suddenly George felt very hungry.

The kitchen door stood open and George walked in.

On the table was a big pot. Of course George was curious.

He had to find out what was in it...

When the cook came back he had a big surprise. Spaghetti was all over the place and in the middle of it was a little monkey!

George had been eating yards and yards and had wound himself all up in it.

The cook was a kind man and did not scold much. But George had to clean up the kitchen and then do all the dishes. My, what a lot of them there were! The cook was watching George. "You are lucky to have four hands," he said. "You can do things twice as quickly.

"I have a friend who could use a handy little fellow like you to wash windows. If you would like to, I will take you over to him."

So they went down into the subway and took an uptown train to the cook's friend, who was an elevator man in a skyscraper.

"Sure, I can use you!" the elevator man said to George. "I will give you what you need for the job. You can start right away. But remember — you are here for washing windows. Never mind what people inside the house are doing. Don't be curious or you'll get into trouble."

George promised to be good, but little monkeys sometimes forget . . .

George was ready to start. My, how many windows there were! But George got ahead quickly, since he worked with all four hands. He jumped from window to window just as he had once jumped from tree to tree in the African jungle.

For a while George stuck to his work and did not pay any attention to the people inside. Of course he was curious, but he remembered his promise.

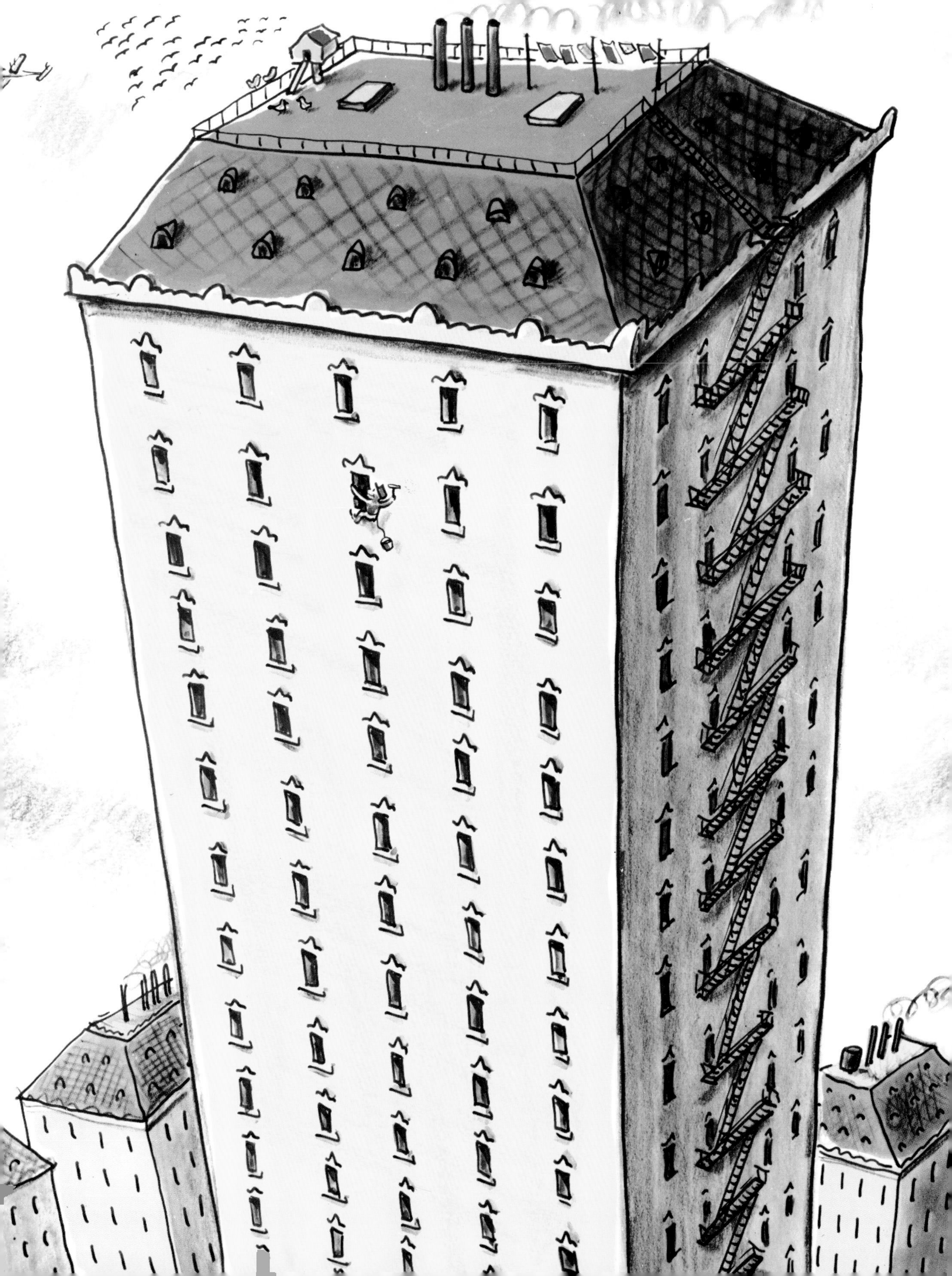

In one room a little boy was crying because he did not want to eat his spinach. George did not even look but went right on with his work.

In another room a man was taking a nap and snoring. George was sorry it was not his friend, the man with the yellow hat. He listened to the funny noise for a while, then went on working.

But what was going on in here? George stopped working and pressed his nose against the window. Two painters
were working inside. George was fascinated. Painting looked
like a lot more fun than washing windows!

The painters were getting ready to go out for lunch. The minute they left George climbed inside.

What wonderful paints and brushes they had! George
could not resist . . .

An hour later the painters came back. They opened the door — and stood there with their mouths wide open. The whole room had changed into a jungle with palm trees all over

the walls and a giraffe and two leopards and a zebra. And a
little monkey was busy painting himself on one of the trees!
Then the painters knew what had happened!

Luckily George was close to a door. He ran out as fast as he could. After him ran the two painters, then the elevator man and then the woman who lived in the place.

"Oh, my lovely room, my lovely room!" cried the woman.

"Don't let him get away!"

George headed for the fire escape.

George reached the end of the fire escape.

The others had not caught up with him yet.

Here was his chance. They could not jump!

But George could easily jump down and escape.

In a moment he would be safe!

Poor little George! He had forgotten that the pavement was hard as stone . . . not like the soft grass of the jungle.

Too bad! The fall broke his leg and an ambulance came to take George to the hospital.

"He got what he deserved!" said the woman "making my apartment into a jungle, indeed!"

"I told him he would get into trouble," the elevator man added. "He was too curious."

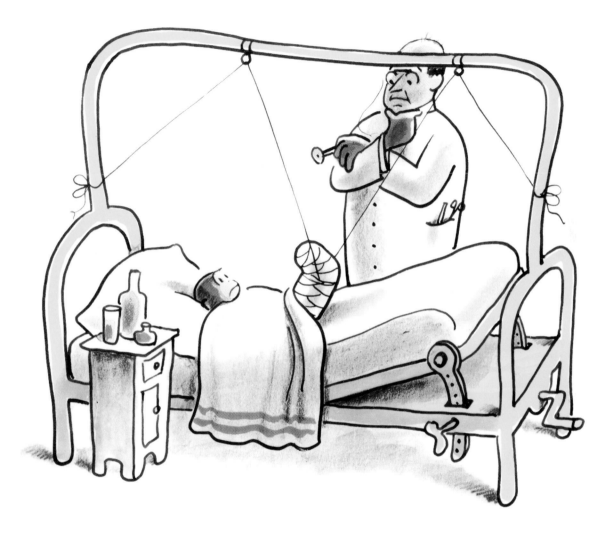

George had to lie in bed with his leg high up in a plaster cast. He was very unhappy.

And it had all started out so nicely! If only he had not been so curious he could have had a lot of fun. Now it was too late . . .

But next morning George's friend, the man with the big yellow hat, was buying his newspaper. Suddenly he got very excited. "This is George!" he shouted when he saw the picture on the front page. Quickly he read the whole story and then ran to a telephone booth to ring the hospital.

"I am George's friend," he said to the nurse who answered the telephone. "Please take good care of him so that he will get better quickly. I want to take him to a movie studio and make a picture about his life in the jungle. Don't let him get into any more mischief until I can take him away."

Finally the day came when George could walk again.

"Your friend is going to take you away this morning," said the nurse. "Just wait right here for him and don't touch anything!"

As soon as George was alone he looked around at all the strange hospital things. "I wonder what is in that big blue bottle," he thought.

George was very curious.

It smelled funny!

Suddenly his head began to turn.

Then he felt as if he were flying.

Then rings and stars danced before his eyes,

then everything went dark...

And this is how the man with

the yellow hat found George when he came to call for him!

They picked him up and shook him but they could not wake

him up. He was so fast asleep that finally they had to put him

UNDER THE SHOWER!

How surprised he was when he woke up!

George said goodbye to the nurse and the kind doctor. Then he and the man with the yellow hat got into the car to drive to the movie studio.

In the president's office George had to sign a contract.
Now he was a movie actor!

In the studio George was kept so busy all the time that he forgot to be curious. He liked the jungle they made for him and played happily there.

And when the picture was finally finished George invited all his friends to see it: the doctor and the nurse and the ambulance driver and the man from the newsstand and the woman and the elevator man and the two painters and the cook and the reporter and all the keepers of the Zoo.

Now the lights went out and the picture started.

"This is George," the voice began.

"He lived in the jungle.

He was a good little monkey —

he had only one fault: he was too curious."

Curious George

rides a bike

This is George.

He lived with his friend, the man with the yellow hat.
He was a good little monkey and always very curious.

This morning George was curious the moment he woke
up because he knew it was a special day . . .

At breakfast George's friend said: "Today we are going to celebrate because just three years ago this day I brought you home with me from the jungle. So tonight I'll take you to the animal show. But first I have a surprise for you."

He took George out to the yard where a big box was standing. George was very curious.

Out of the box came a bicycle. George was delighted; that's what he had always wanted. He knew how to ride a bicycle but he had never had one of his own.

"I must go now," said the man, "but I'll be back in time for the show. Be careful with your new bike and keep close to the house while I am gone!"

George could ride very well. He could even do
all sorts of tricks (monkeys are good at that).

For instance he could ride this way,
with both hands off the handle bar,

and he could ride this way,

like a cowboy on a wild bronco,

and he could also ride backwards.

But after a while George got tired of doing tricks and

went out into the street. The newsboy was just passing by with his bag full of papers. "It's a fine bike you have there," he said to George. "How would you like to help me deliver the papers?"

He handed George the bag and told him to do one
side of the street first and
then turn back and
do the other side.

George was very
proud as he rode off
with his bag.

He started to
deliver the papers
on one side of the street
as he had been told.

When he came to the last house
he saw a little river in the distance.

George was curious: he wanted to know
what the river was like, so instead of turning back
to deliver the rest of the papers he just went on.

There was a lot to see at the river:

a man was fishing from the bridge,

a duck family was paddling downstream,

and two boys were playing with their boats.

George would have liked to stop and look at the boats,

but he was afraid the boys might find out that he had not

delivered all the papers. So he rode on.

While riding along George kept thinking of boats all the time. It would be such fun to have a boat — but how could he get one? He thought and thought — and then he had an idea.

He got off the bicycle, took a newspaper out of the bag
and began to fold it.

First he folded down the corners, like this,

then he folded
both edges up,

brought the
ends together

and flattened
it sidewise.

Then he turned
one corner up,

then the
other one,

again brought
the ends together

and flattened
it sidewise.

Then, gently, he pulled
the ends open —

and there was his BOAT!

Now the moment had come to launch the boat. Would it float? It did!

So George decided to make some more boats. Finally he had used up all the papers and had made so many boats that he could not count them — a whole fleet.

Watching his fleet

sailing down the river

George felt like an admiral.

But watching his fleet he forgot to watch where he was going —

suddenly there was a terrible jolt: the bicycle had hit a rock
and George flew off the seat, head first.

Luckily George was not hurt, but the front wheel of the bicycle was all out of shape and the tire was blown out.

George tried to ride the bicycle, but of course it wouldn't go.

So he started carrying it, but it soon got too heavy.

George did not know WHAT to do: his new bike was

spoiled, the newspapers were gone. He wished he had listened to his friend and kept close to the house. Now he just stood there and cried . . .

Suddenly his face brightened. Why — he had forgotten that he could ride on one wheel! He tried it and it worked.

He had hardly started out again when he saw something

he had never seen before: rolling toward him came an
enormous tractor with huge trailers behind it. Looking out

of the trailers were all sorts of animals. To George it
looked like a Zoo on wheels. The tractor stopped and two

men jumped out. "Well, well," said one of the men, "a little monkey who can ride a bike bronco fashion! We can use you in our animal show tonight. I am the director of the show and this is Bob.

He can straighten your wheel and fix that flat in no time and then we'll take you along to the place where the show is going to be."

So the three of them got into the cab and drove off. "Maybe you could play a fanfare while you ride your bike in the show," the director said. "I have a bugle for you right here, and later on you'll get a green coat and a cap just like Bob's."

On the show grounds everybody was busy getting things ready for the show. "I must do some work now," said the director. "Meanwhile you may have a look around and

get acquainted with all the animals — but you must not feed them, especially the ostrich because he will eat anything and might get very sick afterwards."

George was curious: would the ostrich really eat anything? He wouldn't eat a bugle—or would he? George went a little closer to the cage — and before he knew it

the ostrich had snatched the bugle and tried to swallow it.
But a bugle is hard to swallow, even for an ostrich; it got
stuck in his throat. Funny
sounds came out of the bugle
as the ostrich was struggling with
it, all blue in the face.

George was frightened.

Fortunately the men had heard the noise. They came
rushing to the cage and got the bugle out of the ostrich's throat
just in time.

The director was very angry with George. "We cannot use little monkeys who don't do as they are told," he said. "Of course you cannot take part in the show now. We will have to send you home."

George had to sit on a bench all by himself and nobody even looked at him. He was terribly sorry for what he had done but now it was too late. He had spoiled everything.

Meanwhile the ostrich, always hungry, had got hold of a string dangling near his cage. This happened to be the string which held the door to the cage of the baby bear. As the ostrich nibbled at it the door opened — and the baby bear got out.

He ran away as fast as
he could and made straight
for a high tree near the camp.

Nobody had seen it but
George — and George was not
supposed to leave his bench.
But this was an emergency,
so he jumped up, grabbed the bugle, and blew as loud as he

could. Then he rushed
to his bicycle.

The men had
heard the alarm
and thought at first
that George had
been naughty again.
But when they saw
the empty cage and
the ostrich nibbling
at the string, they knew
what had happened.

George raced toward the tree,
far ahead of the men.

By now the bear had climbed
quite high—and this was dangerous
because little bears can
climb up a tree easily
but coming down
is much harder;

they may fall
and get hurt.
The men were worried.
They did not know how
to get him down safely.
But George had his plan:

with the bag over his shoulder he went up the tree as fast as only a monkey can, and when he reached the baby bear

he put him
in his bag
and carefully
let him down
so that the men
could safely
catch him.

Everybody cheered when George had come down from the tree. "You are a brave little monkey," said the director, "you saved the baby bear's life. Now you'll get your coat back and of course you may ride your bike and play the bugle in the show."

Finally the show was on. The
and how surprised they were
right in the middle of it!
and also the man

whole town had come to see it,
to discover George on his bike
The newsboy was there, too,
with the yellow hat

who had been looking for George everywhere and was happy to have found him at last. The newsboy was glad to have his bag again, and the people from the other side of the street whose papers George had made into boats were not angry with him any more.

George!

When the time had come for George to say goodbye,
the director let him keep the coat and the cap and the bugle.
And then George and his friend got into the car and went . . .

good night!

Curious George

gets a medal

This is George.

He lived with his friend, the man with the yellow hat.

He was a good little monkey — and always very curious.

George was alone this morning, looking at a picture book, when the doorbell rang.

It was the mailman.

"Here is a letter for you," he said. "Put it on your friend's desk. He'll read it to you when he comes home."

George was curious. It was not often that somebody

wrote him. Too bad
he could not read
the letter — but
maybe he could write
one himself! In the
top drawer of the
desk there was paper

and ink and a fountain pen.
George sat down
on the floor
and began to write —
but the pen was dry.

It needed ink; George would have to fill it. He got a funnel from the kitchen and started pouring ink . . .

But instead of going into the pen the ink spilled all over and made a big blue puddle on the floor. It was an awful mess.

Quickly George got the blotter from the desk, but that was no help, the puddle grew bigger all the time. George had to think of something else. Why, soap and water, that's what you clean up with!

From the kitchen shelf he got a
big box of soap powder and poured
all the powder over the ink.

Then he pulled the garden hose through the window,

opened the tap and sprayed water on the powder.

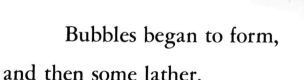

Bubbles began to form,

and then some lather,

and more lather

and more lather

AND MORE LATHER.

In no time the whole room was full of lather,

so full, indeed, that George had to escape in a hurry . . .

When he was safely out of the house he first turned off the tap. But what next? How could he get rid of all the lather before his friend came home?

George sat down in the grass and thought for a long time. Finally he had an idea: he would get the big shovel and shovel the lather out of the window!

But where WAS the lather? While George had been
outside thinking, it had all turned into water. Now the room
looked like a lake and the furniture like islands in it.

The shovel was no use—a pump was what George needed

to get the water out, and he knew just where to find one:
he had seen a portable pump at the farm down the road.

The farmer was away working in the fields. Nobody noticed George when he got the pump out of the shed.

It was heavy. He would need help to pull it all the way back to the house.

Maybe he could tie the goat
to the pump and make her pull it?
But just as George was about to slip
the loop over the goat's head —

he was hurled through the air
and landed near a pen full of pigs.

The biggest pig was standing near the gate. What if George opened the gate just enough to let him out? A big pig could easily pull a small pump.

Carefully George lifted the latch — and before he

knew it, ALL the pigs had burst out
of the pen, grunting and squealing
and trying to get away as fast as they could.
George was delighted. He had never seen anything like it.
For the moment all his troubles were forgotten . . .

But now the pigs were all gone and not a single one was
left to help him with the pump.

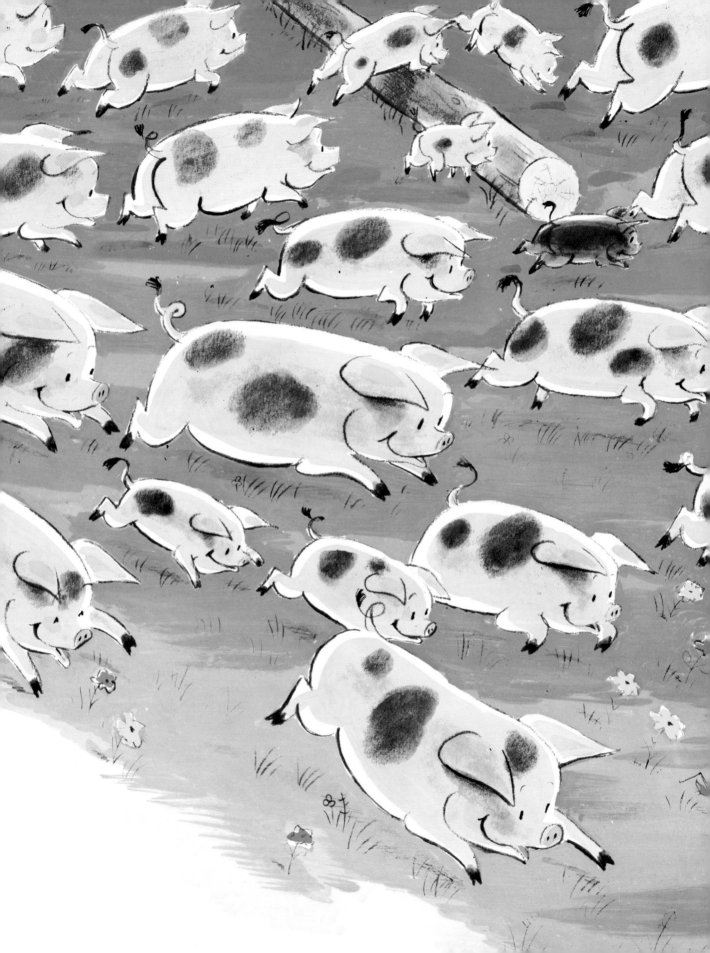

Luckily, there were cows grazing nearby. Cows were gentle and strong. It would mean nothing to a cow to pull the pump for him.

This time George was right, the cow did not mind being tied to the pump. She even let him climb on her back — and off they went! George was glad: now he would soon be home, pump out the room, and everything would be all right.

Meanwhile the farmer and his son had heard the squealing of the pigs. They rushed home from the fields and now had their hands full catching all the pigs. Not until the

last pig was safely back in the pen did they have time to look around. And what did they see? A little monkey riding on their cow, making off with their pump!

The chase was on.
George and the cow
were ahead at first.
But the pump was
slowing them down.
The farmers were getting
closer and closer.

Now they had almost
caught up with them — but
WHERE WAS GEORGE?

Here he was — hiding in a shirt! The farmers had run past him. But on their way home they had to come back over the same road. George did not feel safe in his hiding place . . . Just then a truck came rattling down the road.

George jumped aboard (monkeys
are good at jumping)
and was gone
before the farmers
had a chance
to see him.

The truck drove to a part of town that George had
never seen before. At last it stopped in front of a large
building. It was the Museum. George did not know what a
Museum was. He was curious. While the guard was busy
reading his paper, George slipped inside.

He walked up the steps and into a room full of all sorts of animals. At first George was scared, but then he noticed that they did not move. They were not alive, they were stuffed animals, put into the Museum so that everybody could get a good look at them.

DINOSAUR (EXTINCT)

In the next room George saw something so enormous it took his breath away. It was a dinosaur. George was not scared this time; he knew it was not real. He looked at the dinosaur and then at the baby dinosaur — and then he saw

the palm tree full of nuts. George liked nuts. Suddenly he
felt very hungry (he had missed lunch that day). He would
climb up and . . . Just then he heard footsteps. He had to
hide again — but where?

A family came in to take a look at the dinosaur. They paid no attention to the little monkey who was standing there. The monkey did not move. He stood so still they thought he was just another stuffed animal . . .

George was glad when they were gone! Now he could pick the nuts. He climbed up the dinosaur's neck and started to pull, but the nuts would not come off (George did not know they were not real either). He pulled harder and harder, the tree began to sway . . .

CRASH! Down came the tree on the dinosaur's head, down came the dinosaur, and down came George!

Guards came rushing in from all sides, and underneath the fallen dinosaur they found a little monkey! They pulled him out of there and brought him to Professor Wiseman who

was the director of the Museum. Professor Wiseman was terribly angry. "Lock that naughty monkey up right away," he said, "and take him back to the Zoo. He must have run away from there."

George was carried off in a cage. He felt so ashamed he almost wished he were dead . . . Suddenly the door opened. "George!" somebody shouted. It was his friend, the man with the yellow hat! "It seems you got yourself into a lot of trouble today," he said. "But maybe this letter here will get you out of it. It's from Professor Wiseman; he needs your help for an experiment. I found it on my desk at home — but I couldn't find YOU anywhere, so I came over here to talk to the Professor."

And this is what the letter said:

Dear George,

A small space ship has been built by our experimental station. It is too small for a man but could carry a little monkey. Would you be willing to go up in it?

I have never met you but I hear that you are a bright little monkey who can do all sorts of things, and that is just what we need.

We want you to do something nobody has ever done before: bail out of a space ship in flight.

When we flash you a signal you will have to open the door and bail out with the help of emergency rockets.

We hope that you are willing and that your friend will permit you to go.

Gratefully yours
Professor Wiseman
Director of the Science Museum.

191

"So YOU are George!" Professor Wiseman said. "If I had only known . . . Of course everything will be forgiven, if you are willing to go."

They got the smallest size space suit for George and all the other things he needed for the flight. Then they helped him put them on and showed him how to use them. When everything was ready, a truck drove up with a special television

Check List

☑ 1 Space suit, complete with shoes & gloves

☑ 1 Space helmet

☑ 1 Oxygen tank

☑ 2 Emergency rockets

☑ 1 Parachute

screen mounted on it to watch the flight. They all got on and were off to the launching site. They checked all the controls of the space ship, especially the lever that opened the door. George tried it too.

The great moment had come. George waved goodbye and went aboard. The door was closed. Professor Wiseman began to count: "Five — four — three — two — one — GO!" He pressed the button and the ship rose into the air, slowly first,

and then faster and faster and higher and higher, until they could no longer see it in the sky. But on the screen

they saw George clearly all the time.

Now the moment had come for George to bail out. Professor Wiseman flashed the signal. They watched the screen: George did not move. Why didn't he pull the lever? In a few seconds it would be too late. The ship would be lost in outer space with George in it!

They waited anxiously . . .
At last George began to move.
Slowly, as if in a daze,
he was groping for the lever.
Would he reach it in time?
There — he had grabbed it!
The door opened —
hurrah — George
was on his way!

Out of the blue
an open parachute came floating down to earth. The truck
raced over to the spot where George would land.

What a welcome for George!

Professor Wiseman hung a big golden medal around his neck. "Because," he said, "you are the first living being to come back to earth from a space flight." And on the medal it said: TO GEORGE, THE FIRST SPACE MONKEY.

Then a newspaperman took his picture and everybody shouted and cheered, even the farmer and his son, and the kind woman from next door (who had worked for hours to get the water out of the room).

"I'm proud of you, George," said the man with the yellow

hat. "I guess the whole world is proud of you today."

It was the happiest day in George's life.

The End

Curious George
Flies a Kite

This is George.

He lives in the house

of the man with the yellow hat.

George is a little monkey,

and all monkeys are curious.

But no monkey

is as curious as George.

That is why his name is

Curious George.

"I have to go out now,"
said the man with the yellow hat.

"Be a good little monkey
till I come back.

Have fun and play
with your new ball,
but do not be too curious."

And the man went out.

It was
a lot of fun
for George
to play with
his big new ball.
   The ball
went up,
and George
went up,

and the ball
went down,
and George
went down.

205

George could
do a lot of tricks
with his ball too.
This was one
of the tricks.
He could get up
on the ball like this.

Or do it this way,
with his head down.

This was
another trick
George could do.
He could hold
the ball on his head,
like this.

Look—no hands.
What a good trick!
But—but where did the ball go?

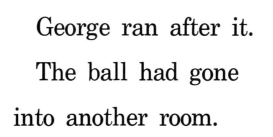

George ran after it.

The ball had gone

into another room.

There was
a big window
in the room.

George liked to look
out of that window.

He could see
a lot from there.

He let the ball go
and looked out.

George
could see
Bill on his bike
and the lake
with a boat
on it.

George
could see
a big house
in a little garden
and a little house
in a big garden.

The big house
was the house
where Bill lived.

But who lived
in the little house?
George was curious.
Who could live in a house
that was so little?

George had to find out,

so he went to the big garden.

The garden had a high wall,

but not too high

for a monkey.

George got up on the wall.

All he had to do now
was jump down—
so George jumped down
into the big garden.

Now he could take a good look
at the little house.

And what did he see?

A big white bunny
and a lot of little bunnies.

George looked and looked and looked.

Bunnies were something new to him.

How funny they were!

The big bunny
was Mother Bunny.

She was as big as George.

But the little bunnies were so little

that George could hold

one of them in his hand,

and that is what he wanted to do.

How could he get a bunny
out of the house?

A house must have a door
to get in and to get out.

But where was the door
to the bunny house?

Oh—there it was!

George put his hand in
and took out
a baby bunny.

216

What fun it was
to hold a baby bunny!
And the bunny did not mind.
It sat in his hand,
one ear up and one ear down
and looked at George,
and George looked back at it.

Now he and the bunny
could play in the garden.

They could play a game.

They could play Get the Bunny.

George would let the bunny hop away,
and then he would run after it
and get it back.

George put the bunny down.

Then he looked away.

One—two—run!

The bunny was off like a shot.

George did not look.

Now he had to wait a little.

One—two—three—four—he waited.

Then George looked up.

Where was the bunny?

He could not see it.

Where was it?

Where had it gone?

George looked for it here,

and he looked for it there.

He could not find it.

Where was the bunny?

It could not get

out of the garden.

It could not get up the wall

the way George could.

It could not fly away.

It had to be here—

but it was not.

The bunny was gone,

and all the fun

was gone too.

George sat down.

He had been a bad little monkey.

Why was he so curious?

Why did he let the bunny go?

Now he could not put it
back into the bunny house
where it could be
with Mother Bunny.

Bad monkey

Mother Bunny—George looked up.

Why, that was it!

Mother Bunny could help him!

George got up.

He had to have some string.

Maybe there was some in the garden.

Yes, there was a string
and a good one too.

George took the string
and went back
to the bunny house.

Mother Bunny

was at the door.

George let her out

and put the string on her.

And Mother Bunny knew what to do.

Away she went
with her head down
and her ears up.
   All George could do was
hold the string
and run after her.

And then Mother Bunny sat down.

She saw something,

and George saw it too.

Something white

that looked like a tail,

like the tail of the baby bunny.

And that is what it was!

But where was the rest of the bunny?

It was down in a hole.

A bunny likes to dig a hole
and then go down and live in it.

But this bunny was too little
to live in a hole.

It should live in a bunny house.

So George got hold
of the little white tail
and pulled the baby bunny out.

Then they all ran back
to the bunny house.

George did not have to put a string
on the baby bunny.

It ran after its mother
all the way home.

George took the string
off Mother Bunny
and helped them back
into the house.

Then Mother Bunny,

and all the little ones

lay down to sleep.

George looked at them.

It was good to see the baby bunny

back where it should be.

And now George would go

back to where he should be.

When he came to the wall,
he could see something funny
in back of it.

George got up on the wall
to find out what it was.

He saw
a long string
on a long stick.
A fat man
had the long stick
in his hand.
What could the man do
with a stick that long?
George was curious.

The fat man was

on his way to the lake,

and soon George was

on his way to the lake too.

The man took a hook
out of his box,
put it on a string
and then put something on the hook.

Then the man let the string
down into the water
and waited.

Now George knew!

The string on the stick
was to fish with.

When the man pulled the string
out of the water,
there was a big fish on the hook.
George saw the man
pull one fish after another
out of the lake,
till he had
all the fish
he wanted.

What fun

it must be to fish!

George wanted to fish too.

He had his string.

All he needed was a stick,

and he knew where to get that.

George ran home as fast as he could.

In the kitchen
he took the mop
off the kitchen wall.
The mop would make
a good stick.
Now George had the string and the stick.
He was all set to fish.

Or was he?

Not yet.

George had to have a hook

and on the hook something

that fish like to eat.

Fish would like cake,

and George knew where to find some.

But where could he get a hook?

Why—there was a hook

for the mop on the kitchen wall!

It would have

to come out.

With the hook
on the string
and the string
on the stick
and the cake
in the box
in his hand,
George went back
to the lake.

George sat down,

put some cake on the hook,

and let the line down into the water.

Now he had to wait,

just as the man had waited.

George was curious.

The fish were curious too.

All kinds of fish came

to look at the line,

big fish and little fish,

fat fish and thin fish,

red fish and yellow fish

and blue fish.

One of them was near the hook.

The cake was just what he wanted.

George sat and waited.

Then the line shook.

There must be a fish on the hook.

George pulled the line up.

The cake was gone,

but no fish was on the hook.

Too bad!

George put more cake on the hook.

Maybe this time

he would get a fish.

But no!

The fish just took the cake

off the hook

and went away.

Well, if George

could not get the fish,

the fish would not get the cake.

George would eat it.

He liked cake too.

He would find another way

to get a fish.

George looked into the water.

That big red one there

with the long tail!

It was so near,

maybe he could get it

with his hands.

George got down
as low as he could,
and put out his hand.

SPLASH!

Into the lake he went!

The water was cold and wet
and George was cold and wet too.
This was no fun at all.

When he came out of the water,

Bill was there with his kite.

"My, you are wet!" Bill said.

"I saw you fall in,

so I came to help you get out.

Too bad you did not get a fish!

But it is good the fish

did not get you."

"Now I can show you how high
my kite can fly," Bill went on.

Bill put his bike up near a tree
and then they ran off.

There was a lot of wind that day,
and that was just what they needed.
The wind took the kite up fast.
George was too little
to hold it in this wind.

A kite that big
could fly away with him.
So Bill had to hold it.
George saw the kite
go up and up and up.
What fun it was to fly a kite!

They let the kite fly

for a long time

till Bill said,

"I will get the kite down now.

I must go home

and you should too."

But when Bill pulled the string in,

the kite got into the top

of a high tree.

Bill could not get it down.

"Oh, my fine new kite!
I can not let go of it.
I must have it back,"
Bill said.
"But the tree
is too high for me."

But no tree
was too high for George.
He went up to the top
in no time.

Then, little by little,
he got the string
out of the tree.

257

Down he came
with the kite
and gave it back
to Bill.

"Thank you, George, thanks a lot,"
Bill said. "I am so happy
to have the kite back.

Now you may have
a ride home on my bike.

I will run back to the lake
and get it.

You wait here for me
with the kite,
but do not let it fly away."

George looked at the kite.

Then he took the string in his hand.

He knew he could not fly the kite
in this wind,
but maybe he could let it
go up just a little bit.

George was curious.

He let the string go a little,
and then a little more,
and then a little more,
and then a little more.

261

When Bill came back,

there was no kite

and there was no George.

"George!" he called.

"Where are you?"

Then he looked up.

There they were,

way up in the sky!

Bill had to get help fast.

He would go to the man

with the yellow hat.

The man would know

what to do.

"George is not here,"
said the man with the yellow hat
when Bill came.

"Have you seen him?"

"George and my kite
are up in the sky
near the lake," Bill shouted.

"I came to . . ."

But the man did not wait
to hear any more.

He ran to his car and jumped in.

"I will get him back," he said.

"I must get George back."

All this time
the wind took the kite up
and George with it.
  It was fun
to fly about in the sky.
  But when George looked down,
the fun was gone.
  He was up so high
that all the big houses
looked as little as bunny houses.
  George did not like it a bit.
  He wanted to get down, but how?

Not even a monkey
can jump from the sky.
George was scared.
What if he never got back?
Maybe he would fly
on and on and on.
Oh, he would never, never
be so curious again,
if just this one time
he could find a way to get home.

Hummmmm—hummmmm.

What was that?

George could hear something,
and then he saw something
fly in the sky just like a kite.

It was a helicopter,

and in the helicopter,

hurrah,

was the man with the yellow hat!

Down from
the helicopter
came a long line.
George got hold of it,
and the man with the yellow hat
pulled him up.
George held on to the kite,
for he had to give it back to Bill.

"I am so happy
to have you back, George,"
said the man with the yellow hat.
"I was scared,
and you must have been scared too.
I know you will not want
to fly a kite again
for a long, long time.
You must give it back to Bill
when we get home."

"Hurrah!" Bill shouted
when George came
to give him the kite.
"George is back,
and my kite is back too!"

And then Bill
took George by the hand
and went with him
into the little garden,

and from the little garden

into the big garden,

where the bunny house was.

"Here is one of my baby bunnies,"
Bill said.

"Take it, it is for you!"

A baby bunny for George!

George took it in his hands

and held it way up.

It was HIS bunny now.

He could take it home with him.

And that is
what he
did.

Curious George

Learns the Alphabet

This is George.

He lived with his friend, the man with the yellow hat. He was a good little monkey, but he was always curious.

This morning George was looking at some of his friend's books. They were full of little black marks and dots and lines, and George was curious: what could one do with them?

The man with the yellow hat came just in time.

"You don't tear a book apart to find out what's in it," he said. "You READ it, George. Books are full of stories. Stories are made of words, and words are made of letters. If you want to read a story you first have to know the letters of the alphabet. Let me show you."

The man took a big pad and began to draw.
George was curious.
"This is an A," the man said. "The A is the first
letter of the alphabet."

A

Now we add four feet and a long tail—
and the A becomes an ALLIGATOR
with his mouth wide open.
The word ALLIGATOR starts with an A.
This is a big A. There is also a small a.
All letters come in big and in small.

This is a small

It looks like a piece of an apple.

George knew alligators and apples.
You could eat apples. Alligators could
eat you if you didn't watch out.

This is a big **B**

The big **B** looks like a **BIRD** if we put feet on it and
a tail and a **BILL**. The word **BIRD** begins with a **B**.
BIRDS come in all colors. This **BIRD** is **BLUE**.
George loved to watch **BIRDS**.

This is a small
It could be a bee.

This bee is busy buzzing around a blossom.
The bee's body has black and yellow stripes.
George kept away from bees.
They might sting, and that would be bad.

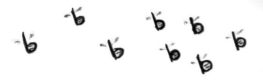

This is a big **C**

We will make it into a CRAB—
a big CRAB,
with a shell, and feet, and two CLAWS.

This is a small **C**

The small c is like the big C, only smaller,

so it becomes a small crab. It's cute.

Crabs live in the ocean.

They can swim or run sidewise and backwards.

Crabs can be funny, but they can also pinch you.

"You now have three
letters, George," the man said,
"A and B and C. With these three letters
you can make a WORD, the first word

you can read yourself. The word is

CAB

cab

You know what a cab is. I once took you
for a ride in a cab, remember? And now
let's draw the next letter."

The big **D**
could be a DINOSAUR.

There are no live DINOSAURS TODAY,
they have DIED out.
Those you see in museums are DUMMIES.
George had seen DINOSAURS in a museum once.

The small **d**
looks like a dromedary.

A dromedary is a camel with one hump.
Riding on a dromedary can make you dizzy because
it goes up and down—up and down—up and down.

desert

The big

is an ELEPHANT.

He is eating his EVENING meal: EGGPLANTS.

George loved ELEPHANTS.

The small **e**

could be the ear of a man,

or the ear of a monkey.
People's ears and monkeys' ears
look very much alike.

The big **F**

is a FIREMAN FIGHTING a FIRE.
Never FOOL the FIRE DEPARTMENT,
or you go to jail, and that's no FUN.

The small **f**

is a flower.

George's friend was fond of flowers.

George preferred food.

The big G

is a GOOSE.

GOOSE starts with a G, like GEORGE

The small g

is a goldfish.

He is in a glass bowl and looks gay.

"Now you know seven letters, George," said the man, "A, B, C, D, E, F, G. With these letters we can already make quite a few words. I have written some of them down: you read them while I get you your lunch."

"It seems the only
word you can read is BAD," said the man when he
came back. "I think we had enough for one morning. I'll feed you now and then you take your nap.
After your nap we'll go on with our letters."

The big **H**

is a HOUSE.

It stands on a HILL behind a HEDGE.

George's HOME used to be the jungle.

Now he lives in a HOUSE.

The small **h**

is a horse.

He is happy because he has heaps of hay.

George had his own horse—a hobby horse.

The big **I**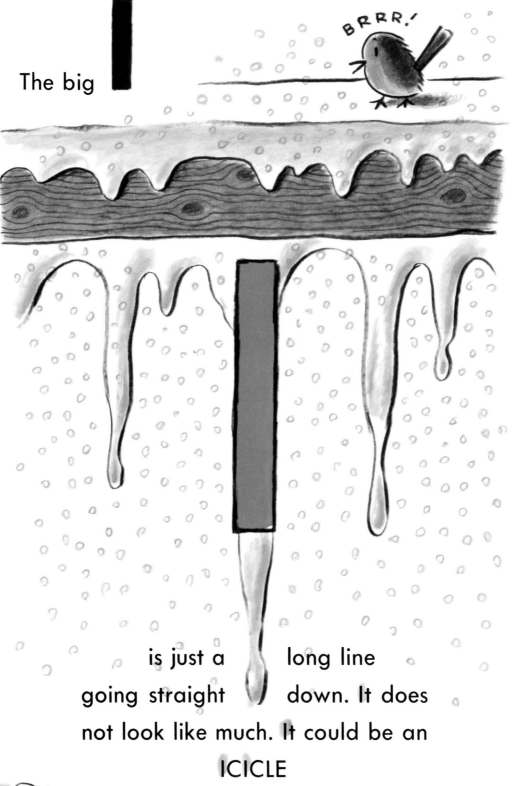

is just a   long line
going straight   down. It does
not look like much. It could be an
ICICLE

The small **i** is a line with a dot on top.
It could be an iguana.

An iguana is a sort of lizard.
Iguanas don't like ice. They like the warm sunshine.
So does George.

The big **J**
is a JAGUAR.

JAGUARS live in the JUNGLE.

George knew JAGUARS.

He had lived in the JUNGLE once.

The small **j**

is a jack-in-the-box.

George had a jack-in-the-box as a toy.

He just loved to make it jump.

The big **K**

is a big KANGAROO called KATY.

The small **k**

is a small kangaroo.

He is Katy's kid.

The big **L**

is a LION.

He is LUCKY. He is going to have

LEG of LAMB for LUNCH, and he LOVES it.

The small **I**

is a lean lady.

She is strolling along a lake licking a lollipop.

George liked lollipops.

The big **M**

is a MAILMAN.

His name is MISTER MILLER. He brings a letter.

Maybe it's for ME, thinks George.

The small **m**

is a mouse.

He is munching mints.

"And do you know what else it is?" said
the man to George: "M is the thirteenth letter
of the A B C. The whole alphabet has only

26 letters, so thirteen is just half of it. You can make lots of words with these letters. Why don't you try? Here's a pad and pencil."

George started to think of words, and then he wrote them down. It was fun to make words out of letters.

"Let me see," said the man. "Ball – Milk – Cake – Ham – Jam – Egg – Lime – Feed – Kid – that's very good.

But what on earth is a Dalg or a Glidj or a Blimlimlim? There are no such things. Just ANY letters do not make words, George.

Well, let's look at some new letters now."

The big **N**

is a NAPKIN

standing on a dinner plate. It looks NEAT.

George had seen NAPKINS folded that way

in the restaurant when he was a dishwasher.

The small **n**

is a nose
in the face of a man.
He has a new blue necktie on
and is nibbling noodles.

The big  is a big OSTRICH,

and the small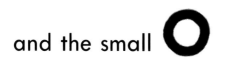

is a small ostrich, of course.

Ostriches eat odd objects.
One ostrich once had tried to eat a bugle
that belonged to George.

The big P

is a big PENGUIN,

and the small **p** is a small penguin.

These penguins live near the South Pole.
They use their flappers as paddles.
George knew penguins from the Zoo.

PLOP!

The big **Q**

is a QUAIL.

QUAILS have short tails.

You must keep QUIET if you want to

watch QUAILS. They are quite shy.

The small **q** is a quarterback.

A quarterback has to be quick. George was quick. He would qualify for quarterback.

"And now get your football, George," said the man, "it will do you good to play a little before we go on with your letters."

George knew how to play the game. He knew how to carry the ball,

and how to take a three-point stance,

and how to get ready for the kick-off.

He was a fine halfback, too,

and he could make a short pass,
or recover a fumble.

"Good game," said the man, "but
time's up now: back to the alphabet!"

The big **R**

is a RABBIT.

Some RABBITS are white with RED eyes.

RABBITS love RADISHES.

George loved RABBITS. He had one as a pet.

The small **r**

is a rooster.

The rooster crows when the sun rises.

Two roosters will start a rumpus.

They really can get rough.

329

The big **S**

is a big SNAIL,

and the small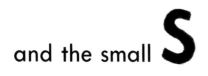

is a small snail.

Snails are slow. They sneak into their shells

when they are scared of something.

George thought snails looked silly.

The big **T**

is a TABLE.

The TABLE is set for TWO. It is TIME for TEA.

George did not care for TEA,

but he liked TOAST.

The small  is a tomahawk.

George had a toy tomahawk.
It was a tiny one.
He took it along when he played Indian.
He also had a tepee—an Indian tent.

"Now it's time for a snack," said the man. "Run over to the baker, George, and hand him this note. Then come right back with the doughnuts, one dozen of them, and no tricks, please!"

George was curious. He looked at the note the man had written. One dozen doughnuts . . . Maybe he could write something on it too? How about writing TEN instead of ONE? He had just learned the T . . . First a T— then an E—then an N . . .

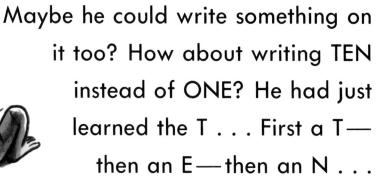

"Hmm," said the baker, "ten dozen doughnuts is quite a lot, but that's what the note says. We need an extra-big bag for them."

"Why, George!" cried the man. Then he saw the note. "Well, that comes from teaching the alphabet to a little monkey. And I told you: no tricks!"

TEN ONE DOZEN DOUGHNUTS

336

"You may not eat any
doughnuts now, George.
Put them back in the bag
and let's go on with
the letters!"

U

The big **U**
is a big **U**MBRELLA
standing **U**PRIGHT.

The umbrella handle
is also
like a **u**.

George knew how to **U**SE an **U**MBRELLA.

The small **U**
is a small umbrella.

When it is raining umbrellas are useful
but you must keep under the umbrella
unless you want to get wet.
George thought rain was a nuisance.

The big **V**

For George
from the man
with the
yellow
hat

is a big **V**ALENTINE,

and the small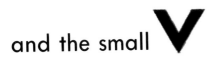

to George
with
Love
*

is a small valentine.

George loved valentines.

He got several valentine cards every year.

One card came from Nevada.

The big  **W** and the small **W**
are WHISKERS, big ones and small ones.

A WALRUS has WHISKERS.

Some men  have whiskers

and cats have whiskers.

George did not have whiskers
but he was curious how
he would look if he did.

The next letter of the alphabet is X.

The big **X** and the small **X** look alike, only one is big and one is small, just like the big W and the small w, or the V, or the U, or the S, and some of the other letters.

"BUT," said the  man, "there are few words that start with an X, and they don't look like an X—

except one, and that is Xmas!"

Santa stands for Xmas.

There is only one Santa so we need only one picture.

George thought Xmas was exciting.

The big **Y**

is a big YAK

and the small Y

is a small yak: he is still young.
Yaks live in Tibet. If you haven't seen any yaks yet
you may find one at the zoo.

The big **Z**

is a big ZEBRA,

and the small **Z** is a small zebra.

The zebras are zipping along with zest.

"And do you know what?" said the man, "Z is the last letter. Now you know all the 26 letters of the alphabet—

and NOW you may have the doughnuts."

Curious George

Goes to the Hospital

IN COLLABORATION WITH THE CHILDREN'S HOSPITAL MEDICAL CENTER, BOSTON

This is George.

He lived with his friend, the man with the yellow hat. He was a good little monkey, but he was always curious.

Today George was curious about the big box on the man's desk.

What could be in it? George could not resist.
He simply HAD to open it.

It was full of funny little pieces of all sorts of
shapes and all sorts of colors.

George took one out.
It looked like a
piece of candy.

Maybe it WAS candy. Maybe he could eat it. George put the piece in his mouth—and before he knew, he had swallowed it.

A while later the man with the yellow hat came home. "Why, George," he said, "I see you have already opened the box with the jigsaw puzzle. It was supposed to be a surprise for you. Well, let's go to work on it."

Finally the puzzle was finished—
well, almost finished.
One piece was missing.

The man looked for it everywhere, but he could
not find it. "That's strange," he said, "it's a brand-
new puzzle. Well, it cannot be helped. Maybe
we'll find it in the morning. Let's go to bed now,
George."

The next morning George did not feel well. He had a tummy-ache and did not want to eat his breakfast.

The man was worried. He went to the telephone and called Doctor Baker. "I'll be over as soon as I can," said the doctor.

First Doctor Baker looked down George's throat and felt his tummy. Then he took out his stethoscope and listened. "I'm not sure what's wrong," he said. "You'd better take George to the hospital and have an X-ray taken. I'll call them and let them know you are coming."

"Don't worry, George," said the man when they were driving to the hospital, "you have been there before, when you broke your leg. Remember how nice the doctors and nurses were?"

George held his big rubber ball tight as they walked up the hospital steps.

A nurse took them down a long hallway to a room where she gave George something to drink that looked white and tasted sweet. "It is called barium," the nurse explained. "It helps the doctors find out what is wrong with you, George."

In the next room stood a big table, and a doctor was just putting on a heavy apron. Then he

gave the man one just like it. George was curious:
Would he get one too? No, he did not.

"You get on that table, George," the doctor
said. "I am going to take some X-ray pictures of
your insides." He pushed a button and there was
a funny noise. "There—now you may get up, and
we will have the X-rays developed right away."

"Now let's see . . . There is something there that should not be," said the doctor when they were looking at the X-rays.

"Why, that looks like . . . I think that must be the piece that was missing in our jigsaw puzzle yesterday!" said the man. "Well, well, well," said the doctor, "at least we know now what is wrong with our little patient. I'll tell Doctor Baker right away. George will have to stay at the hospital for a few days. They'll put a tube down his throat to get the piece out. It's only a small operation. I'll call a nurse and have her take you to the admitting office."

Many people were waiting outside the office.
George had to wait too.

"Look, Betsy," the woman next to him said to her
little girl, "there is Curious George!" Betsy looked up
for a moment, but she did not even smile. Betsy had
never been to a hospital before. She was scared.

Finally it was George's turn.

A pretty young nurse took him to the next room —my, how many rooms and how many nurses there were! One nurse wrote down a lot of things about George: his name and his address and what was wrong with him. Another nurse put a bracelet around his wrist. "It has your name on it, George," she said, "so that everybody knows who you are."

Then the pretty young nurse came back. "My name is Carol," she said. "I am going to take you to your room now—we call it the children's ward —and put you to bed. There will be lots of children to keep you company."

And so it was. There were a lot of children in
the room. Some were up and around; others were
in their beds, with a doctor or a nurse looking
after them.

Dave was having a
blood transfusion. Steve had his leg bandaged
and was sitting in a go-cart. Betsy was in bed
looking sad. George got the bed next to Betsy.

George was glad when he
was in his bed at last. His tummy
was hurting again.

The man sat with him for a while. "Now I have
to leave you, George," he finally said. "I'll be
back first thing in the morning before they take you
to the operating room.
Nurse Carol will tuck
you in when it's time
to sleep."

Then he left. George
just sat there and cried.

As he had promised, the man was back early next morning. The nurses were keeping George very busy. One nurse was taking his temperature; one was taking his blood pressure; one was giving him a pill ("To make you sleepy, George," she said), and one was getting ready to give him a shot.

"It's going to hurt, George," she said, "but only for a moment."

She took his arm, and George let out a scream.

"But the needle hasn't touched you yet," said the nurse, laughing. "There—now it's done. That wasn't so bad, was it?"

No, it really was not.

And anyway, it was

over now.

By the time the attendant came with the stretcher to wheel him to the operating room, George was getting sleepy. He tried hard to stay awake. He was curious to see what would happen next.

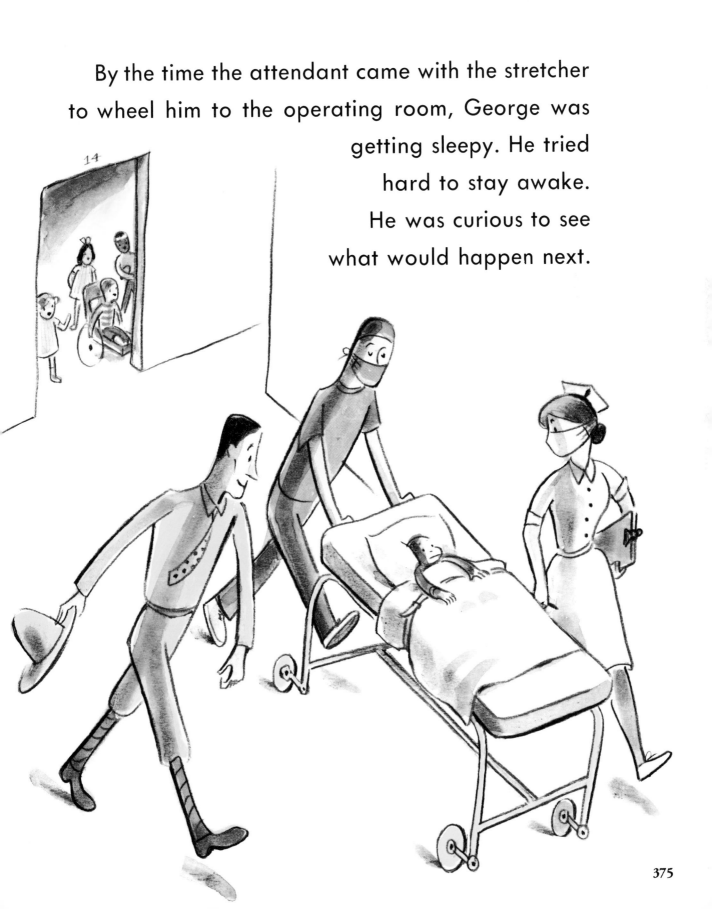

He could see a big table with bright lamps over it and doctors and nurses all around. They had caps on their heads and masks over their faces; only their eyes were showing.

One of the doctors winked at George and patted his head. It was Doctor Baker, who had

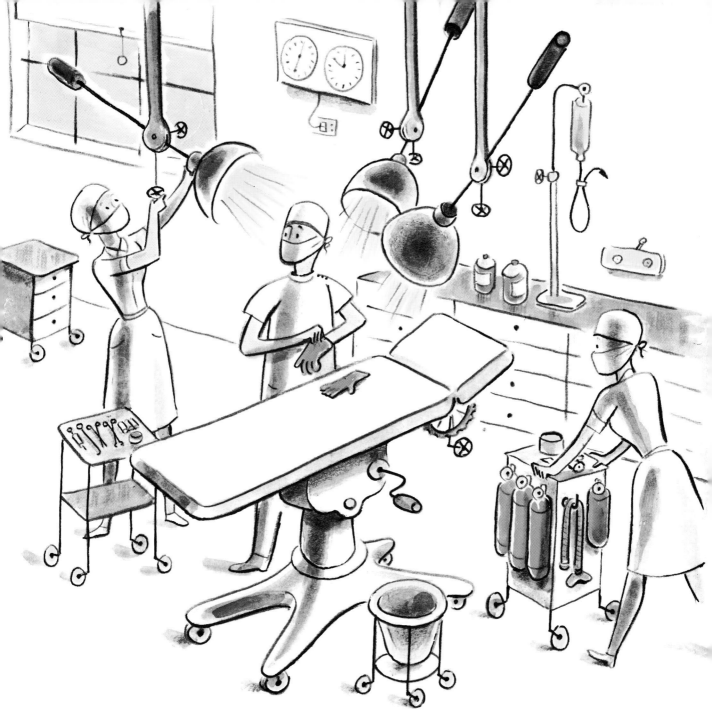

been to the house when it all had started. He
looked funny with his mask on...And then George
was fast asleep.

When George woke up he did not know what
had happened. He did not even know where he
was. Then he saw Nurse Carol. "It's all done,
George," she said. "They got the piece out. In a
day or two you will be running around again."

The man had brought him a picture book. But
George felt sick and dizzy. His throat was hurting,
too. He was not even curious about the new book.
He closed his eyes again. "We'll let him sleep,"
said Nurse Carol. "The more he sleeps, the better."

The next morning George felt better. He even ate a dish of ice cream. Dr. Baker came to see him, and the man, of course, came too.

Betsy was watching him from time to time. She seemed a little less sad, but she still did not smile.

Steve wheeled his go-cart over to George's bed. "Tomorrow I can get up and try to walk," he said. "Boy, I can hardly wait."

"I'll take you to the playroom now, George," Nurse Carol said the next morning, "and in the afternoon your friend will come and take you home."

The playroom was full of children. A lady was showing Betsy how to use finger paint. There were all sorts of things to play with, even a puppet theater—and that was just the thing for George. He had four hands so could handle four puppets at the same time.

George gave
a real puppet show,
with a dragon
and a clown
and a bear
and a policeman.

The children laughed
and shouted,
and even Betsy
for the
first time
smiled a little.

There was a TV set in the playroom and also a record player. George was curious: If he climbed on the record player
and turned the switch,

would it go round
and round like a
real merry-go-round?

It did!
It started slowly,
then it went faster and
faster, and whoopee!
George had lost his
balance and was
sailing through the air...

Luckily George landed on a soft cushion. The children cheered, and Betsy smiled again. George was SO funny.

But then the play lady picked George up. "That's enough for now," she said. "You'd better take a nap before lunch. We have a big day ahead of us. The mayor is coming to visit the hospital today, and later on you will be going home, George."

When George woke up,

Steve was just taking his first steps.

A nurse was helping him, and the children were

watching.

The go-cart was standing there empty.

George was curious.

He looked at it.

Then he climbed

into it.

Then he grabbed
the wheels and then, while
nobody was looking, he wheeled the go-cart right
out of the room.

George
could make
the go-cart go very fast.
This was fun! Down the hall he went.
By now the nurse had noticed that he
was gone and came running after him.
"George! George!" she shouted.

But George was
too excited to listen.
He wheeled around the corner
and down the ramp to the floor below,
where some men were busy pushing
lunch carts, and a lot of doctors and

nurses were showing the mayor around.

George tried to stop,

but it was too late.

WHAM!—the go-cart landed

right in the middle of everything.

Lunch carts tumbled. Spinach and scrambled eggs and strawberry jam were all over the floor. People fell over each other, and George was thrown out of the go-cart and landed right in the mayor's arms.

What a mess it was!

"You broke all my dishes!" someone cried.

"He ruined the go-cart!" complained another.

"What will the mayor think of it?" whispered someone else. And so it went.

Suddenly everybody looked up and listened. From above came happy laughter—and there stood Betsy, laughing, laughing, laughing. Then the children joined in, then the mayor started laughing, and finally everybody just laughed and laughed. Everybody, that is, except George.

Betsy came running down the ramp, threw her arms around George, and kissed him. "Don't be sad, George," she said. "The whole thing was SO funny! I never laughed so much in my life. I'm so glad you were in the hospital with me."

Now the director of the hospital spoke: "I am sorry this happened, Mr. Mayor," he said, "but I think we'll just clean up the mess and be done with it."

"George," he went on, "you've made a terrible mess. But you also made our sad little Betsy happy again, and that is more than any of us has done.

"And now I see your friend has just come to take you home. So, goodbye George, and take good care of yourself."

The children
crowded around the
windows waving goodbye when
George and the man with the yellow
hat were finally leaving the hospital.

As the car was turning into the driveway Nurse Carol came running after them. "Here's a little package with something that belongs to you, George," she called. "But don't open it before you are home!"

George was curious—
well, who would not be?
The moment he reached home
he ripped the paper off,
tore open the box—
and THERE

was the piece
of the puzzle
that had caused
all the trouble!

"How nice of the doctor to save it for us!" said the man with the yellow hat. "And NOW we can finish the puzzle."

The End

Retrospective Essay

by Dee Jones
WITH A PHOTOGRAPHIC ALBUM OF MARGRET AND H. A. REY

Early Life

Both Hans and Margret Rey were born in Hamburg, Germany—Hans Augusto Reyersbach on September 16, 1898, and Margarete Elisabeth Waldstein on May 16, 1906. Hans received an old-style humanistic education and studied Latin, Greek, French, and English. Although art was not a part of his studies, he loved to draw and did so from a very young age. A drawing of horses in the park was done when he was just eight years old.

Hans, better known by his initials, H.A., served in the German army during World War I and was stationed in France and Russia. In the early 1920s, H.A. and Margret met at a party at her parents' house in Hamburg. He was dating her older sister at the time, and when he first saw Margret she was sliding down the banister.

In 1924, due to the increasing inflation in Germany, H.A. moved to Rio de Janeiro, Brazil, to work as an accountant in his brother-in-law's import-export firm. Among other duties, he sold bathtubs

401

and kitchen sinks up and down the Amazon River for twelve years. The surname of "Rey" was adopted by H. A. when the Brazilians began to address him using the shortened form of his tongue-twister name.

Meanwhile, Margret was still in Germany, where she received formal art training at the Bauhaus in Dessau in 1927, when Paul Klee and Wassily Kandinsky were on the faculty. She also studied at the Düsseldorf Academy of Arts from 1928 to 1929 and held one-artist shows of her art in Berlin in the early 1930s. Margret worked for a British advertising agency in Berlin, where she wrote the lyrics to the first jingle for a radio commercial for Lever Brothers margarine. She also worked as a professional photographer in Berlin and London before moving to Rio de Janeiro in 1935.

Advertising Art

Upon arriving in Rio, Margret became reacquainted with H. A. Rey and persuaded him to leave his brother-in-law's firm. Together they founded the first advertising agency in Rio de Janeiro. They were married on August 16, 1935. They created stories for newspapers and magazines with Margret's writing and H. A.'s illustrations. Margret also continued her photography, and H. A. found steady work with Hoffmann–La Roche, a pharmaceutical firm. He produced many of their direct mail advertising campaigns, utilizing witty illustrations. He also drew maps and posters, illustrated cookbooks, and designed Christmas cards for corporate clients.

Early Books

Margret and H. A. took a belated honeymoon trip to Europe, and their planned two-week stay in Paris turned into four years. During that happy time, H. A. began to write and illustrate books. *Zebrology,* published by Grace Hogarth at Chatto & Windus in London in 1937, is Rey's first title in English, although not a children's book. *How the Flying Fish Came into Being,* a wordless book consisting of eight illustrated panels, followed in 1938. That year also saw the publication of *Le Zoo* and *Le Cirque,* toy books complete with paper animals to punch out and assemble. An editor at Gallimard saw Rey's whimsical drawings of a giraffe in a French periodical and suggested that he make them into a children's book. Thus was born *Rafi et les 9 Singes,* published in 1939. An English-language version was also published the same year by Chatto & Windus as *Raffy and the 9 Monkeys.* Raffy's name was changed to Cecily G. (G. for giraffe, of course) in the subsequent American edition. French children loved the antics of one of the nine monkeys named "Fifi" and begged for more stories about him. Fifi was soon renamed "George" and went on to fame and fortune in his own series of books.

Curious George

In June 1940, on a rainy morning before dawn, the Reys left Paris on bicycles just hours before the Nazis entered the city. They took only warm coats and their manuscripts and artwork—among the stories was *Curious George.* After selling their bicycles at the French-Spanish border, they went by train to Lisbon, on to Rio de Janeiro, and finally arrived in New York City in October

1940. Grace Hogarth, who had published their books at Chatto & Windus and was now at Houghton Mifflin, soon acquired *Curious George,* which was published in 1941. *Curious George* slowly became a classic throughout the world, and editions have appeared in every possible language, with George renamed "Zozo," "Bingo," "Nicke," "Coco," and "Piete," among others.

Music Books

In the early 1940s, H. A. Rey began a series of delightful music books, utilizing traditional French children's songs, Mother Goose rhymes, and Christmas carols. They are *Au Clair de la Lune* (Greystone, 1941), *Humpty Dumpty and Other Mother Goose Songs* (Harper, 1943), *We Three Kings* (Harper, 1944), and *Mary Had a Little Lamb and Other Nursery Songs* (Puffin, 1949). Rey's creativity is evident in these books, in which he replaced the traditional designation of whole, half, quarter, and eighth musical notes with a symbol pertinent to the song.

Books Written by Others

Although H.A. and Margret Rey almost always wrote and illustrated their books together, H.A. illustrated several books for other authors that were published by Harper and Brothers during the 1940s. Rey was fortunate to work with legendary editor Ursula Nordstrom, and together they created several original books. *Goodnight Moon* author Margaret Wise Brown collaborated with Rey on two books, *The Polite Penguin* in 1941 and *Don't Frighten the Lion* in 1942. Other collaborations, all published in 1944, included *Katy No-Pocket,* by Emmy Payne; *Egbert and His Marvelous Adventures,* by Paul T. Gilbert; and *The Park Book,* by Charlotte Zolotow. *Don't Frighten the Lion* was originally titled "Monkey Business," but the title was changed because Rey had promised his editors at Houghton Mifflin that he would not create books with other publishing firms that would directly compete with their Curious George books. A paper doll and clothing designed by Rey were printed inside the front cover of *Don't Frighten the Lion*.

Elizabite

Another early H.A. Rey title edited by Ursula Nordstrom is *Elizabite,* published in 1942. Rey's delightful sense of humor takes center stage in this book about a carnivorous plant. From the jacket flap copy comes the following description: "When asked about the origin of *Elizabite,* Mr. Rey (who has spent many years in Brazil) told of an evening in Rio when he was dining with friends, among them a botanist who entertained the party with strange tales about carnivorous plants. Ever since, Mr. Rey has looked with suspicion at flower arrangements on dinner tables, and, as the years went by, he often tried to imagine what a carnivorous plant might develop into, under proper care. His thoughts on the subject crystallized into the colorful and energetic shape of Elizabite in the present book."

Tit for Tat

Tit for Tat is an inventive turnabout tale of what would happen if animals did unto us as we do unto them. It was a hit with children and adults alike, as evidenced by the following quotations. From a letter to the Reys from editor Ursula Nordstrom we learn, "The salesmen are all in happy hysterics over *Tit for Tat,* and so is everyone who has seen the original dummy—the man at *Publishers Weekly,* for instance." A review in the December 1943 *Junior Reviewers* relates that "a kindergarten group greeted this with screams of laughter, and you could see the enjoyable visions it started in the darling little heads, such as one comment, 'Oh boy, if I could only play tit for tat with my father!'"

Toy Books

At the same time that Harper and Brothers was publishing *Elizabite* and *Tit for Tat,* Houghton Mifflin was busy with several "cut-out-and-play" books created by Uncle Gus. Uncle Gus was, of course, Hans AuGUSto Rey, and his *Christmas Manger, Uncle Gus's Circus,* and *Uncle Gus's Farm,* all published in 1942, were instant successes. A May 3, 1942, piece in the *New York Times Book Review* comments, "The elephants and monkeys and clowns of *Uncle Gus's Circus,* the pigs and horses and cows . . . of *Uncle Gus's Farm* will push out of the page . . . all ready to stand up when folded. . . . These ingenious books have real charm and will provide solid enjoyment and relief for both children and parents on a long train journey or when a child is ill enough to stay in bed but not too ill to be amused."

Le Zoo, another toy book created by Rey, was published in 1938 by Hachette in France. Since its design was unique, it was protected by a patent rather than the traditional copyright.

Pretzel

Pretzel was the first book on which Margret Rey's name appeared as author. She often provided ideas and edited the text and illustrations created by her husband, but this was the first time that she actually received credit for her creativity. In the concluding pages of the story, Pretzel finally captures the heart of Greta; they marry and have a litter of five puppies. The sequel, *Pretzel and the Puppies,* consists of a series of two-page stories presented in a picture strip format similar to that of a comic strip. These short stories also appeared in *Good Housekeeping* magazine in the late 1940s. A balloon replica of Pretzel was featured in a Macy's Thanksgiving Day Parade.

Katy No-Pocket

What is a kangaroo to do when she has a baby but no pocket? Author Emmy Payne teamed up with illustrator H. A. Rey to provide an exceptional solution to the problem in *Katy No-Pocket* (1944). Rey explained his creative process for *Katy No-Pocket* in the Junior Literary Guild's monthly magazine for its young readers, *Young Wings:* "When I have an idea that seems to me just right for a book, I make sketches and jot down a few words and show them to the boys and girls who are my friends. They tell me what they think and give me very useful suggestions. This showing of my book-in-the-

making to my small friends is quite a necessary test, for I am usually so fond of my own ideas that I want to put everything into the book."

Billy's Picture

Billy's Picture was published by Harper and Brothers in 1948 and was so popular that it was reprinted in Danish, Swedish, German, and Japanese. Despite this worldwide acceptance, the United States sales began to sag in the late 1960s. Upon receiving a royalty statement in 1966, the Reys thought *Billy's Picture* must be out of print because the sum was so small! Following the adage that a picture is worth a thousand words, H.A. wrote a letter to Ursula Nordstrom at Harper, asking about the book's status. On the letter was a drawing of a tombstone reading "Here Lies Billy, 1948–1965, R.I.P.," with a reclining rabbit in the grass. At the Reys' insistence, Billy was resuscitated with a reprinting of the book using a different color scheme.

The Stars

H.A. Rey was so intensely interested in astronomy that he took a star guide along with him when he served as a German soldier in World War I. He found most guides impossible to interpret and vowed someday to create a more understandable method of constellation recognition. That he did in 1952 with the publication of *The Stars: A New Way to See Them*, the work of which was triggered by the design of the Reys' 1947 New Year's card, which featured a constellation motif. H.A. spent more than four years creating *The Stars*, an immediate best-seller. It has since become the definitive star-watching guide, popular with laymen and professionals alike, and is still in print. Many adults who know nothing of *Curious George* are very familiar with H.A. Rey's name because of *The Stars*. He later published a children's version entitled *Find the Constellations*.

Curious George Sequels

After the publication of *Curious George* in 1941, fans had to wait another six years before more adventures of the mischievous monkey appeared in *Curious George Takes a Job*. The Reys often made cameo appearances in their books—in this second title of the series, on page 13, one can find Margret with her dog and H. A. with a friend promenading on Fifth Avenue. The third title, *Curious George Rides a Bike,* was published in 1952. In this series of misadventures, George "sets off on his new bicycle to deliver newspapers, . . . builds a whole navy of paper boats, lands in a traveling circus, . . . gets an ostrich into trouble, and rescues a runaway bear."

In the fourth title, *Curious George Gets a Medal,* published in 1957, George goes up in a spaceship and receives a medal for his bravery. Two years later, the

United States launched a squirrel monkey named Gordo into space aboard *Jupiter AM-13*. Gordo was followed in 1959 by Able and Baker, who rode in a nose cone to an altitude of 300 miles and a distance of 1,500 miles. It seemed clear to Margret Rey that their fictional story had inspired the actual events.

Since it was issued as part of a beginning-reader series, *Curious George Flies a Kite* was written with a restricted vocabulary of only 219 words. According to author Margret Rey, "It was a fad then, and many educators thought first-graders could learn to read quicker that way. Like so many things, it proved to be nonsense and was given up after a while. Luckily, children never noticed that this book was written differently from the other Curious George books."

Margret recalled some difficulty in preparing the British edition of *Curious George Learns the Alphabet*. "You might think the British use the same alphabet as we do. Far from it! Several pictures had to be changed. . . . No 'Xmas' there, no 'mailman' (it is 'postman' in England), no 'quarterback,' no 'truck' (it is 'lorry' in England), and so on. So we had to find substitutes."

The final *Curious George* book written during H. A. Rey's lifetime is *Curious George Goes to the Hospital*. The story line was suggested to the couple by administrators of Children's Hospital in Boston. They wanted a book to pre-

He got off the bicycle, took a newspaper out of the bag and began to fold it.

First he folded down the corners, like this—

The small ✝

is a turtle.
You can keep turtles in a tub as pets, they get quite tame. If you tease a turtle he pulls his head and feet and tail into his shell.

pare children for their first visit to a hospital. The Reys derived a great deal of satisfaction from this book, since many mothers wrote to tell them how effective it was in reducing their child's trauma.

Whiteblack the Penguin

"Whiteblack the Penguin," never published in the Reys' lifetime, has vibrant full-color illustrations and is complete with beautifully hand-lettered text. According to correspondence in the archive, it was submitted for publication to Ursula Nordstrom of Harper and Brothers. In a letter dated October 27, 1942, Nordstrom commented, "I think Whiteblack can be shortened, sharpened, and improved. I hope you will let me see it again." There is no written evidence that the manuscript was resubmitted. It remained in the Reys' possession and was transferred to the de Grummond Children's Literature Collection at the University of Southern Mississippi, where the entire Rey archive is housed. There, in the fall of 1999, Anita Silvey, publisher of children's books at Houghton Mifflin, discovered the manuscript. *Whiteblack the Penguin Sees the World* was finally published in 2000.

New Year's Cards

The Reys had a tradition of designing and producing an original card each year to mail to family and friends. They used the cards to inform people of a new address, to comment on the world political situation, or to showcase an imaginative idea.

This is George. He lived in Waterville Valley. He was a Baby Squirrel. The Scrimshaws' cat caught him (but he was not hurt) and Susan Scrimshaw brought him To us, on Sunday, August 6, 1967. He was with us for two weeks, fed with an eye dropper. He died August 20. He had a short but happy life, and was fun to have around.

Waterville Valley

Although very much at home in their Greenwich Village apartment, the Reys wanted to spend summers in the country, where Margret could garden and H. A. could have a clear view of the heavens. On May 14, 1958, construction began on the Curious George Cottage in Waterville Valley, New Hampshire. Here they spent relaxing summers and drew inspiration from their bucolic existence there. H. A. was well known for rescuing injured animals and nursing them back to health. Coffee, an orphaned chipmunk whom H. A. had hand-fed with an eyedropper and returned to the wild, came back each summer to visit his human friends. Another benefactor of H. A.'s tender care was George the squirrel, whose watercolor image drawn by Rey is shown above.

Other Artwork by Margret

Margret had many interests and accomplishments. She was fluent in four languages and, in addition to writing and editing, she spent her early adult years as a journalist and photographer. When she and H. A. were first married, she put her considerable skills to work supplying newspapers and magazines with photographs.

Another outlet for Margret's creativity was pottery. She trained at the Haystack Mountain School of Crafts in Deer Isle, Maine, in the late 1960s and early 1970s. She designed and created decorative pieces, as well as functional teapots, bowls, plates, and cups. Among the decorative items are two versions of Jonah and the whale, Aztec-inspired women carrying baskets, a mother elephant and her baby, a pair of dragon candleholders, and two whimsical figures that represent Margret and her husband.

Needlepoint was yet another creative outlet for Margret. She designed, charted, and stitched a number of complex images over the years. Among her needlepoint works are a portrait of H. A. with Curious George in the background, an unfinished self-portrait, a footstool depicting Scoopy (the Reys always had a cocker spaniel, and Scoopy was their third dog), a portrait of Andy (spaniel number four), Jonah and the whale, and a picture of the Washington Square apartment where they lived from 1941 to 1949.

Stuffed Georges

The first stuffed Curious George was produced by Commonwealth Toys in 1971. Margret and H.A. took great pains to ensure that the stuffed toys were accurate representations, with eyes and nose correctly spaced and sized and with the correct colors used in the fur. Various Curious Georges range in height from six inches to six feet. A jogging George was introduced by Knickerbocker Toys in 1982 and came complete with a hooded sweatshirt.

Merchandising

In addition to the stuffed versions of Curious George, there are hundreds of products bearing his image: photo albums, lunch boxes, sweatshirts, and wash-cloths. There are View-Master reels, rolls of stickers, wooden puzzles, Magic Slates, Colorforms, tennis shoes, a china music box, and a Curious George board game.

Personal Greetings

H.A. was well known for creating personalized greetings for his wife and other relatives and friends. Included in the archive are several original birthday cards given to Margret. The Reys were rarely apart, but, when Margret attended pottery classes in Maine for several weeks each summer from 1969 to 1972, H.A. remained in Waterville Valley. He sent heavily illustrated letters to Margret almost every day, keeping her in touch with his activities.

The following group of photographs provides a visual history of the personal and professional lives of Margret and H. A. Rey. These and many other photographs are a part of the Rey archive housed at the University of Southern Mississippi.

LEFT:
H.A. Rey proudly displaying the cover of Whiteblack the Penguin Sees the World, *late 1930s*

BELOW:
Margret and H.A. Rey relaxing in Rio de Janeiro, where they briefly lived in the summer of 1940 before moving to New York

SINAIS PESSOAIS—SIGNALEMENT

		Espôsa—Femme
Profissão / Profession	Desenhista	Fotógrafo
Estado civil / Etat civil	casado	casada
Lugar e data do nascimento / Lieu et date de naissance	Alemanha 16-9-1898	Alemanha 16-5-1906.
Domicílio / Domicile	Rio de Janeiro	Rio de Janeiro
Rosto / Visage	oval	oval
Côr dos olhos / Couleur des yeux	azues	azues
Côr do cabelo / Couleur des cheveux	castanho	castanho. claro
Sinais particulares / Signes particuliers	calvice	———

FILHOS—ENFANTS

Nome—Nom	Idade—Age	Sexo—Sexe

Portador—Porteur *Assinatura do portador* *Signature du porteur*

Espôsa—Femme *Assinatura de espôsa* *Signature de sa femme*

Passports issued to H. A. and Margret Rey by the Brazilian Consulate in New York, 1942

H. A. Rey looking out over the New York City landscape from the Reys' apartment window, early 1940s. Photo probably taken by Margret

H. A. Rey with cocker spaniel Charkie, 1944

Margret Rey with cocker spaniel Charkie, 1944

H. A. and Margret Rey pose for the camera in the late 1940s

H.A. and Margret Rey, 1951

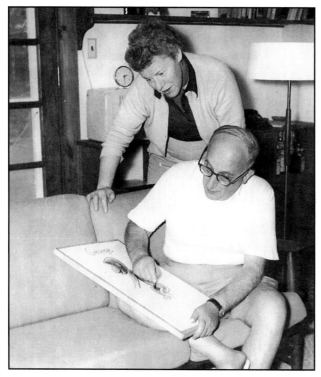

Margret Rey as art director, Waterville Valley, New Hampshire, 1954

Margret Rey and cocker spaniel Jamie, circa 1956

H.A. and Margret Rey work on Curious George Flies a Kite *with Charles Rheault of Riverside Press at Houghton Mifflin, 1958*

Ambidextrous H.A. with Margret on the book tour for Spotty, *St. Louis, 1958*

H.A. Rey working in his studio, early 1960s

The Reys promoting Curious George Goes to the Hospital, *1966*

H. A. Rey reading to children in the 1970s

H. A. Rey with friend

Margret Rey surrounded by Curious George replicas on the occasion of her ninetieth birthday, 1996

H. A. Rey the astronomer